CLASSIC TALES

# PETER PAN

Alexis Roumanis

www.av2books.com

Your AV² Media Enhanced book gives you a fiction readalong online. Log on to www.av2books.com and enter the unique book code from this page to use your readalong.

# AV² Readalong Navigation

Go to **www.av2books.com**, and enter this book's unique code.

## BOOK CODE

**A 4 8 3 2 3 5**

AV² by Weigl brings you media enhanced books that support active learning.

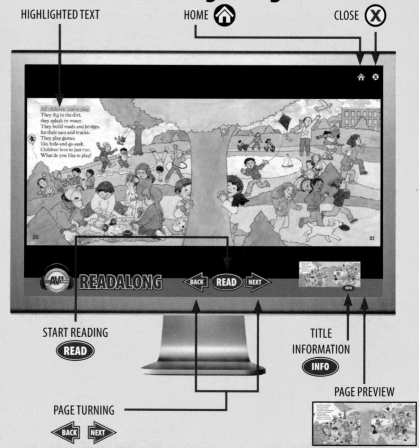

HIGHLIGHTED TEXT

HOME

CLOSE

START READING
READ

PAGE TURNING
BACK NEXT

TITLE INFORMATION
INFO

PAGE PREVIEW

Published by AV² by Weigl
350 5ᵗʰ Avenue, 59ᵗʰ Floor New York, NY 10118
Website: www.av2books.com

Library of Congress Control Number: 2016930579

ISBN 978-1-4896-5248-5 (Hardcover)
ISBN 978-1-4896-5250-8 (Multi-user eBook)

Copyright ©2008 by Kyowon Co., Ltd.
First published in 2008 by Kyowon Co., Ltd.

Printed in the United States of America in Brainerd, Minnesota
1 2 3 4 5 6 7 8 9 0  20 19 18 17 16

032016
012916

2

There once was a girl named Wendy.

Wendy shared a bedroom with her younger brothers, John and Michael.

Their dog, Nana, was very protective of Wendy and her two brothers.

Nana was always on guard.

One night, a boy named Peter Pan came to Wendy's window.

He was followed by a glowing fairy that made a tinkling sound as she flew.

Nana heard the tinkling sound
and bolted to the window.

"Let's get out of here, Tinkerbell!"
cried Peter to the fairy.

Peter was about to escape through the
window when Nana caught his shadow.

"Let go!" yelped Peter.

Nana pulled so hard
that Peter's shadow fell off.

Peter and Tinkerbell flew to safety.

Later that night, Peter snuck
back into Wendy's room.

"I must get my shadow back," sobbed Peter.

He found his shadow sitting on the dresser.

"What are you doing over there?"
Peter asked his shadow.

Peter grabbed his shadow by the foot,
but couldn't get it to follow him.

Just then, Wendy walked
into the room and gasped.

7

"What are you doing in my room?"
asked Wendy in shock.

"I lost my shadow," said Peter.
"I can't get it to come with me."

"I have never seen someone lose their
shadow before," said Wendy.
"Maybe I can help you."

Wendy got a needle and some thread, and
began to sew Peter's shadow to his shoe.

"I think that's done it," said Wendy proudly
when she had finished.

"Thank you!" beamed Peter.

Just then, Wendy's brothers
walked into the room.

"Would you like to come to
to Neverland with me?" asked Peter.
"It's the magical land where I live."

"I can't leave without my brothers," said Wendy.

"They can come, too," said Peter merrily.
"Tinkerbell, sprinkle fairy dust on them
to help them fly."

The small fairy flew over Wendy and her brothers.
As she flew, glowing sparkles fell over them.

"In order to fly, you have to think of something
happy," encouraged Peter.

They all thought of something happy.
Soon, all four of them were floating
in the air.

"Follow me!" Peter said.

After a long flight,
Wendy could see a small island below.

"This is Neverland," said Peter happily.

"Is that a pirate ship?" asked John.

"Yes," replied Peter. "That's Captain Hook's ship."

"Why is he called Hook?" asked Michael.

"A crocodile ate his hand," said Peter. "Now he has a hook, instead of a hand."

Suddenly, the pirate ship fired a cannon ball.

"Fly away!" screamed Peter.

Wendy flew away from the pirate ship in a panic.

She forgot to follow Peter and was soon
lost in the forest.

"Where am I?" she wondered.

Suddenly, an arrow flew towards Wendy.

"Help!" cried Wendy, falling to the ground.

Peter heard Wendy's cry and came to help.

"What happened, Lost Boys?" yelled Peter.

"I thought she was a giant bird," said one of the boys.

"Is she hurt?" sobbed Tinkerbell.

Peter saw a small tear on the side of Wendy's nightgown.

"I don't think you actually hit her," said Peter hopefully. "She just got scared and fainted."

Peter picked Wendy up and carried her to his home.

Wendy joined her brothers
at Peter's house.

"We were worried about you," said John.

"I'm okay, but I am very tired,"
replied Wendy. "We should go to bed."

"Can we hear a bedtime story first?"
asked Michael.

"Of course, dear," replied Wendy.

Wendy told them a story about a beautiful
mermaid. When she was finished,
everyone fell fast asleep.

The next day, Peter took everyone to the beach.

"I want to show you real mermaids," said Peter.

When they arrived, they saw pirates
standing on the rocks.

"Oh no!" gasped Peter. "The pirates captured the
island princess, Tiger Lily!"

Peter snuck up behind the pirates.

"Let her go!" boomed Peter.

The pirates were so surprised
that Tiger Lily was able to break free.

"It's Peter Pan!" boomed Captain Hook. "Capture him!"

"You've never been able to catch me before," yelled Peter, pulling out his sword.

John, Michael, and the Lost Boys kept the other pirates at bay.

"It looks like it's just you and me, Hook," taunted Peter.

The Captain tried to catch Peter with his hook, but Peter was too quick.

There was a loud splash in the water.

"Look behind you," yelled Peter.
"It's the crocodile!"

"Do you think I would fall for such a
simple trick?" laughed Hook.

"Captain, it really is the crocodile!"
yelled one of the pirates.

Hook's face turned pale with fear.

"Run away!" cried Hook.

Everyone was exhausted when they returned
to Peter's hidden underground house.

"Wendy, can you tell us another story?"
asked one of the Lost Boys.

"Tell us about your parents," said another.

"My parents are kind and loving," said Wendy.
"Every night they tuck me into bed with a kiss."

"Do you think they are worried about us?"
asked Michael.

"They are probably awake right now, waiting
for us," said Wendy.

"Peter, is someone back home
worried about you?" asked John.

"No, I am an orphan," said Peter flatly.
"I have no parents."

"How did you get here?" asked John.

"One day, I went fishing, and there was
a terrible storm," explained Peter.
"I fell into the water and nearly drowned."

"Oh no!" cried Michael. "How were you saved?"

"A large bird pulled me out of the water,"
said Peter.

"We sailed to Neverland together
on the bird's floating nest."

"You are very lucky to have parents waiting for you back home," said Peter.

"Our parents won't forget about us, will they?" asked John.

"We won't become orphans, will we?" sobbed Michael.

"No, dears," said Wendy softly. "Our parents will wait for us."

"We should go home now," urged John.

"Yes," said Michael. "I want to go, too."

"Okay," said Wendy. "Let's ask Tinkerbell
to take us home."

"I thought you would want to stay here,"
said Peter. "Don't you want to live
with me in Neverland?"

"I'm sorry, Peter, we cannot. You can come back
with us, though," offered Wendy.

"Please come," said John. "You can live with us."

"No, if I leave Neverland I will start
to grow up," said Peter.

"I want to be a boy forever."

Just then, Tinkerbell flew into the room.

"What's wrong?" asked Peter.

"It's Hook," said Tinkerbell worriedly.
"He has found our underground house."

"Oh no!" said Wendy. "What will we do?"

"He has us surrounded," said Tinkerbell.
"There is no way we can escape."

"There must be something
we can do," Wendy said worriedly.

"I have one idea," said Tinkerbell quickly.
"Peter, you can drink this sleeping potion."

"How will that help us?" asked one
of the Lost Boys.

"Captain Hook will think you are dead,"
said Tinkerbell. "When he captures us, he
will leave you behind."

"Then, you can come rescue us," said John.

"I will try," said Peter.

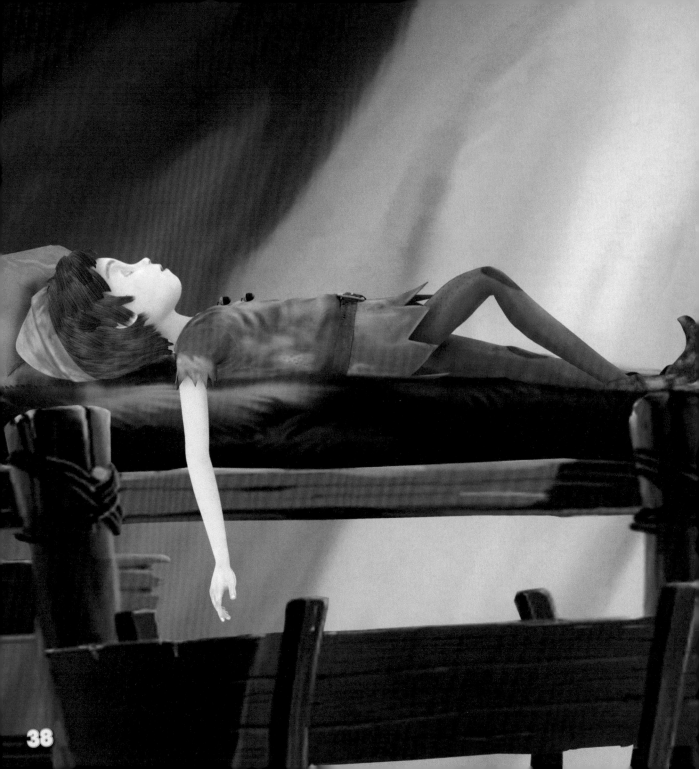

Peter drank the potion and fell fast asleep.

When Hook arrived, he took everyone captive.

"What happened to Peter Pan?"
bellowed Hook.

"He fell in the water and drowned,"
sobbed Wendy, pretending to be upset.

When everyone was gone,
Tinkerbell woke Peter up.

"Hurry," said Tinkerbell.
"We must save them!"

Peter and Tinkerbell flew to
Hook's ship as fast as they could.

Peter landed right behind Wendy.

"Hi Wendy," he whispered with a wink.

"Thank goodness you're here," said Wendy softly.
"They are about to throw John off the ship."

"Walk the plank, boy," Hook shouted to John.

"Watch this, Wendy," said Peter quietly.

In a deep, booming voice, Peter shouted,
"The crocodile is on the ship!"

"Everyone off the ship, now!"
ordered Hook in fright.

The pirates jumped into the water
and swam for shore.

The crocodile, who always stayed near the ship,
noticed Captain Hook in the water.

It turned toward Hook hungrily.

The children watched as the crocodile
chased Captain Hook far from the ship.

"You saved us!" John cried.

"Thanks to Tinkerbell," said Peter, beaming at her.

"Can we fly home now?" asked Michael.

Tinkerbell sprinkled fairy dust on everyone
and they began to float

"Let's go!" encouraged Peter.

Peter and Tinkerbell flew home
with Wendy and her brothers.

"That was fun," exclaimed Michael,
clapping his hands.

"Thank you!" Tinkerbell said, making joyful
tinkling sounds.

"Every time you clap your hands,
a fairy comes to life."

"Peter, you can stay with us, if you want,"
said Wendy.

"No thanks. There are too many adventures for
me out there," replied Peter happily.

Then, Peter Pan and Tinkerbell waved good-bye
and flew back to Neverland.

As the years went by,
Wendy never forgot about Peter Pan.

She became a teacher, and told the story
of Peter and Tinkerbell to every child she met.

She always finished her story by repeating
what Tinkerbell had told her.

"Whenever you clap your hands, a fairy
comes to life," Wendy would say.

Her students would clap their hands
and dream of going to Neverland
one day themselves.

**Sir James Matthew Barrie** was born in 1860 in Kirriemuir, Scotland. He attended the University of Edinburgh where he wrote reviews for the *Edinburgh Evening Courant*, and graduated with a Master of Arts degree. He worked as a journalist after graduating and later wrote magazine stories, plays, and many novels.

Peter Pan's first appearance in literature was as a character in Barrie's 1902 adult novel, *The Little White Bird*. Barrie liked the character so much that he rewrote *Peter Pan* as a play in 1904. The novel was first published under the title *Peter and Wendy* in 1911.